EP)

Who Needs Birds When DOGS Can FLY?

FAY ROBINSON

Photographs by CHARLES R. SMITH Jr.

DUTTON CHILDREN'S BOOKS • NEW YORK

"The Walk" first published in The Bark magazine, Spring 2002, issue 18
"Car Ride" first published in The Bark magazine, Winter 2000, issue 10

Library of Congress Cataloging-in-Publication Data
Robinson, Fay.
Who needs birds when dogs can fly?/by Fay Robinson; photographs by
Charles R. Smith Jr.—1st ed.
p. cm.
Summary: Humorous poems and photographs celebrate the special
relationships between children and their dogs—from the canine point of view.
ISBN 0-525-47019-0 (Hardcover)
1.Dogs—Juvenile poetry. 2.Children's poetry, American.
[1. Dogs—Poetry. 2. American poetry.] I. Smith, Charles R., 1969- ill.
II. Title.
PS3568.O2887 W48 2002
811'.54—dc21 2002002590

Published in the United States 2002
by Dutton Children's Books,
a division of Penguin Putnam Books for Young Readers
345 Hudson Street, New York, New York 10014
www.penguinputnam.com

Designed by Irene Vandervoort
Printed in Hong Kong
First Edition
1 3 5 7 9 10 8 6 4 2

To great dogs everywhere,
who live every day as though it is their birthday.
With special appreciation to Sydney, Kiko, Sophie, Feegba,
Niki, Ozzie, and Maude.
F. R.

For P. Butter and T. Bear
C. R. S. Jr.

Wake Up!

Hot breath, cold nose, wet tongue:

DOG IN YOUR FACE!

I lick you awake.

My eyes shimmer brighter
than birthday candles.
On hip-hopping feet,
with my tail wagging wild,
you know what I'd say if I could speak:

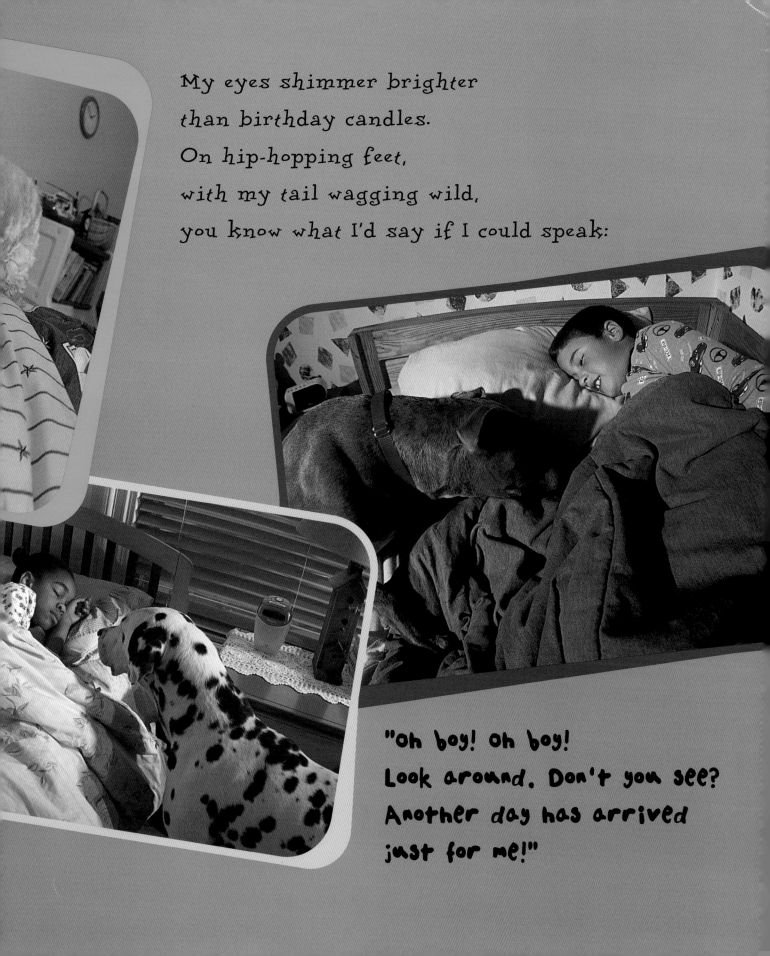

"Oh boy! Oh boy!
Look around. Don't you see?
Another day has arrived
just for me!"

Belly
Rub

You pat my head
and stroke my neck.
"Good dog, good dog.
You are the best."
While many might be satisfied,
I am reminded that a belly rub
would feel better.
I flop on my back,
then guide your hand
with my front feet
till you reach that soft spot
just below my chest.

Good boy, good boy.
You are the best.

Breakfast

On your mark, get set, go!

I plunge my nose into the bowl

and gulp my food—

no need to chew.

Because I'm so smart,
I know I must beat you
to these delicious bits of...
of...
What IS this stuff?
No time to decide.
I suck in the last crumb
and, full to the brim,
look left, look right.

I win!

When You Leave

How dare you leave without me?
I look at you with pleading eyes
and flump in a lump on the floor.

So sad, so sad,

head pressed to the ground,
brow furrowed in furry wrinkles.
If dogs cried tears, I'd shed a few.

And if I do this right,
I know that when you're out,
you'll feel terrible, too.

WHILE YOU

WERE GONE

You look around

and your home is a-flutter

with pieces of paper and feathers.

Shredding the *Times* was fun,

but fighting the pillow was better.

The smell of bird was almost more

than any dog could bear.

It was a marvelous hunt.

Too bad
you weren't
there.

The Couch

I own the couch.

It is my throne.

I ascend,

fold my feet beneath me,

and sink my chin into a cushion.

You look around

and your home is a-flutter

with pieces of paper and feathers.

Shredding the *Times* was fun,

but fighting the pillow was better.

The smell of bird was almost more

than any dog could bear.

It was a marvelous hunt.

Too bad
you weren't
there.

When You Return

I run laps around the dining room table,

snortling with glee at each pass.

Finally I stop to dance at your feet,

prancing and smacking

your calves with my nose

till you get on your knees

and kiss me back.

The Couch

I own the couch.

It is my throne.

I ascend,

fold my feet beneath me,

and sink my chin into a cushion.

Eyes closed, I dream
of roaming mighty forests,
unearthing log-sized bones.

I open one eye
when you tell me to scat,
then shut it again
because I am a dog,
and *this* is my throne.

WINDOW STREAKS

I love to look out the window,
(or that's what you think).
While watching the sights,
the feel of cool glass
on my wet nose
brings out the artist in me.

Soon the window is smudged
with nose strokes
and nasal drips
in half-moons and flowing lines.
And when the design is just right,
I leave.

The Walk

I pull you wildly down the street,
pointing out the cool things
with my nose:
fence posts, cat-sized stones,
squirrel trails, mystery holes,

chewed-up sticks and chicken bones,
and dogs, children, DOGS!
Bounding with bliss—
if I could wish for anything in life,
it would be this.

Beggar

I wait at your feet
when you eat anything
(even a grape)
and stare it down like prey.
If it doesn't jump into my mouth,
I put my head on your knee
and lift my eyes to yours.
They say, I haven't eaten in months,
and grapes just like these,
even if I spit them out,
would quench a hunger unlike
anything you've ever known.
Please?

Watchdog

The mail comes.

The doorbell rings.

A neighbor's dog goes out.

All reasons to bark

as loudly and incessantly

as a fire alarm.

I can't stop I can't stop I can't stop
till the coast is clear.
You never know
when someone might need
to be reminded about
just who is in charge of this house.

Car Ride

The window must be open wide—
I hang my body half outside
and breathe the wind,
taste the sky,
size up the whole neighborhood
all in one whiff.
Fur and ears flattened,
I squint into the rush
of the world flashing by.

Who needs birds when dogs can fly?

Bedtime

I jump onto your bed,
count three circles around,
and curl into a heap at your feet.
You must not disturb me as I sleep,
for, although I have napped
on and off all day,

my sleep is more important than yours.
So you lie bunched
in your half of the bed
while I snore the soft snores
of a dog at the end
of the very best day of its life,
again.

Sydney ⬆

⬇ Leya

AUTHOR'S NOTE

This book was inspired by my two dogs, one past and one present. Leya, my maniac husky, pulled me wildly down the streets for fourteen years. She successfully guarded the house against squirrels and neighboring dogs with the world's loudest bark. Her favorite activities were running, digging (the lawn or, when necessary, the carpet), running, slaying pillows, and running.

Sydney is my gray mutt—half keeshond, half bear cub, as far as anyone can tell. Among the things she likes best are snow, broccoli (her favorite food), and belly rubs. She took ownership of the couch shortly after she moved in and is currently working on tearing up the cushions.

—FAY ROBINSON

PHOTOGRAPHER'S NOTE

Photographing four dogs with four kids in four homes was a monumental task. To get the dogs to do what I wanted, I used a lot of treats and lots of peanut butter. In the photos where the dogs had to be close to the kids, such as the "Wake Up!" shots, I put peanut butter behind the kids' ears to get the dogs to pay attention. The kids hated peanut butter on their ears, but the dogs loved it. The experience I had photographing a dog for one of my previous books, Loki & Alex, was also a tremendous help.

In the end, everything came together to show the fun between kids and their dogs and that's what this book is all about. Enjoy!

—CHARLES SMITH